H A T S

Devised and illustrated by

Clare Beaton

WARWICK PRESS

Contents

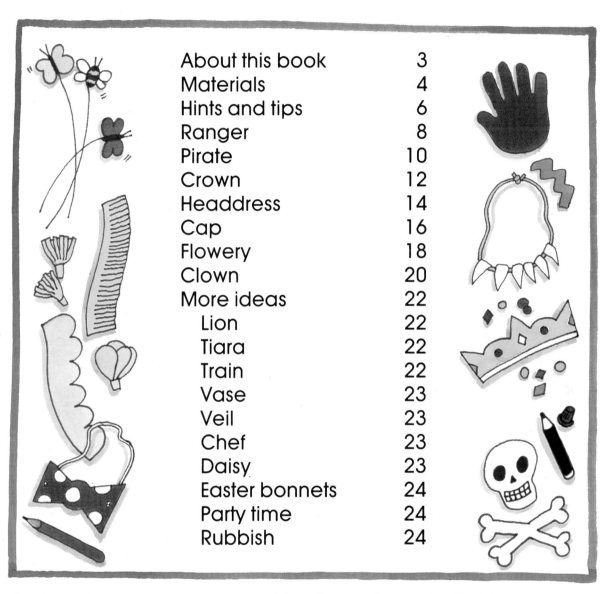

Produced by
Tony Potter, Times Four Publishing Ltd

Published by Warwick Press, 387 Park Avenue South,
New York, New York 10016, in 1990
Paperback edition published by Franklin Watts,
387 Park Avenue S., NY, NY

First published in 1990 by Grisewood & Dempsey Ltd,
London.

Copyright © 1990 Times Four Publishing Ltd.
All rights reserved.

Typeset by TDR Photoset, Dartford
Colour separations by RCS Graphics Ltd
Printed in Spain

Conception and editorial:
Catherine Bruzzone, Multi Lingua

Library of Congress Cataloging-in-Publication Data

Beaton, Clare.
  Hats / Clare Beaton.
    p. cm. – (Make and play)
    Summary: Describes the materials required for making hats, and
provides patterns of popular hat designs.
    ISBN 0-531-15162-X   ISBN 0-531-19097-8 (lib. bdg.)
    1. Hats – Juvenile literature. [1. Hats. 2. Handicraft.]
I. Title. II. Series. III. Series: Beaton, Clare. Make and play.
TT657.B43 1990
646.5–dc20   89-2152
                                                       C
                                                       A

93-934

About this book

This book will show you some easy and fun ways to make hats. There are step-by-step instructions for seven main hats and ideas for lots more at the end of the book.

On the left-hand pages, there are four simple steps to follow:

On the right-hand pages, there is the finished hat with some extra suggestions for you to try:

The simplest hats are at the beginning of the book and the more complicated ones at the end. You should be able to find most of the materials you need in your home. Look at pages 4-7 for some helpful hints.

You can make the easiest hats very quickly but will need to plan, and perhaps shop, for some of the others. The extra hats at the end of the book do not have step-by-step instructions but most can be made in similar ways to the main hats.

Warning

With this book, older children should be able to make all but the most complicated hats on their own. However, they may need adult help occasionally and younger children will need help and supervision. It is worthwhile teaching children to use tools such as craft knives correctly and safely right from the start. Take

special care with tools like scissors, knives, and staplers and use non-toxic children's glue and paint. Craft knives with blades which retract into the handle are recommended, as are round ended-scissors.

Take extra care where you see this symbol: ⚡

Materials

Keep a box of oddments that can be used to make things: cardboard boxes and packages, cardboard tubes, sticks, feathers, beads, buttons material, papers, doilies, string and anything colorful and decorative. You could buy old hats, net curtains, lacy material, scarves, old jewelry and so on, at sales and in junk shops.

Keep ribbons and trimmings from presents and candy boxes.

Even the boxes may come in useful.

Felt is wonderful to use. It doesn't fray and comes in lots of brilliant colors. You can sew it or glue it.

Look out for feathers, dried leaves, and grasses when you are out for a walk. If you need a lot of feathers, try asking at a farm or a butcher's.

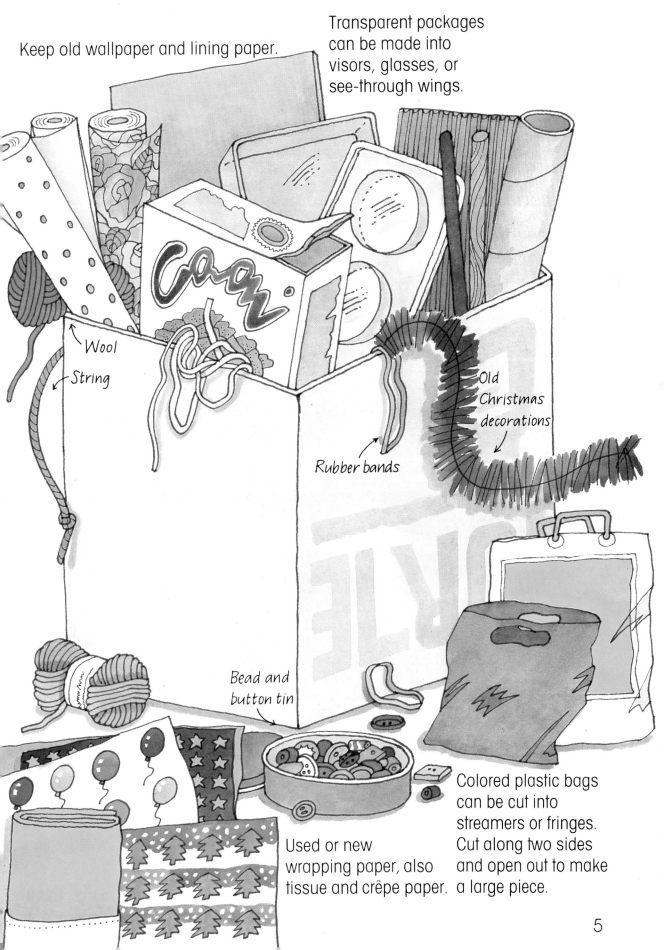

Keep old wallpaper and lining paper.

Transparent packages can be made into visors, glasses, or see-through wings.

Wool

String

Rubber bands

Old Christmas decorations

Bead and button tin

Used or new wrapping paper, also tissue and crêpe paper.

Colored plastic bags can be cut into streamers or fringes. Cut along two sides and open out to make a large piece.

Hints and tips

A sewing basket will have lots of things you need, such as scissors, pins, needles and thread. Don't forget to ask the owner first, before you begin! It's a good idea to build up your own store of different kinds of elastic, buttons, ribbon, braid, safety pins and anything decorative and fun that might come in useful.

A small stapler is very useful for joining things, such as thin elastic to card (instead of sewing) or a band of paper or card (instead of using sticky tape). Do make sure that the staple ends are closed properly and don't leave staples lying around.

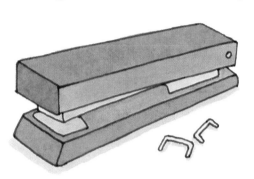

Elastic

Staple

Staple

Pinking shears are scissors that cut with a zigzag to stop material from fraying. They are also useful because they make a pretty edge.

A paper hole puncher is also useful and fun to use. You can use one to make patterns.

A sewing machine is useful but is not essential and is best used only by an adult. Hand sewing will do fine.

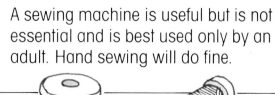

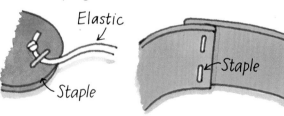

Pattern of holes

Keep drawing things together where you can find them easily. Look after them carefully and they will last longer and work better. Always keep paper flat. It takes time to flatten out a roll of paper.

Don't forget to put a newspaper on the table or floor before you start.

Keep stickers safe in a bag.

Use an old plate to mix colors.

ickers

Wash brushes carefully in between colors and when you have finished. Don't leave them in the water as this makes the bristles soften and bend. Change the water often when you paint.

Put the tops on paints after you have used them.

Cut this way

Other hand holds things to be cut.

Always put tops on pens so that they don't dry out. Throw old ones away.

When cutting out with a craft knife, ALWAYS have some cardboard or best of all a piece of lino or hardboard underneath so you don't cut the table! With tricky cutting it's best to get an adult to help.

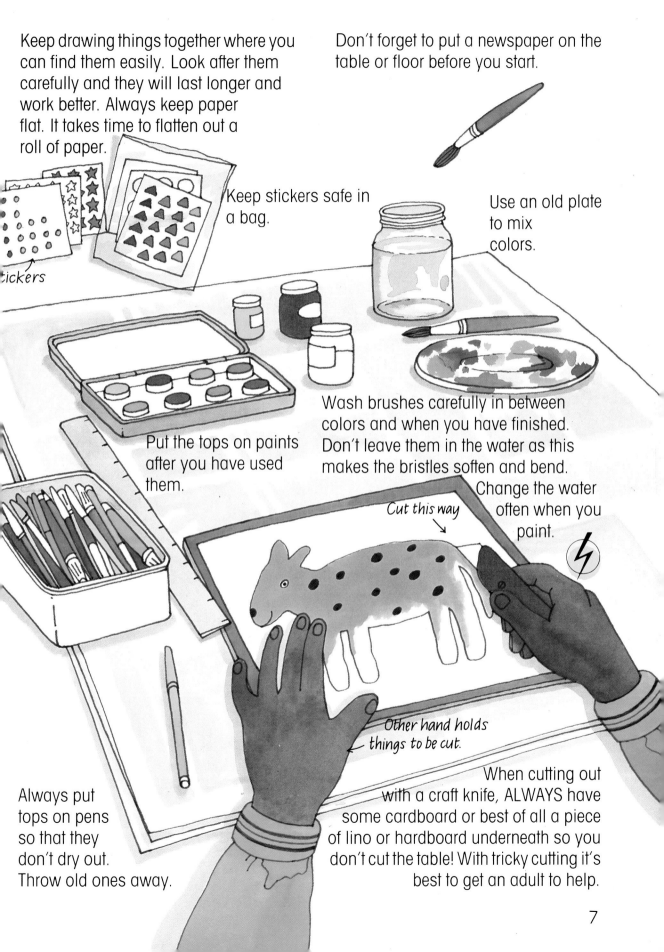

Ranger

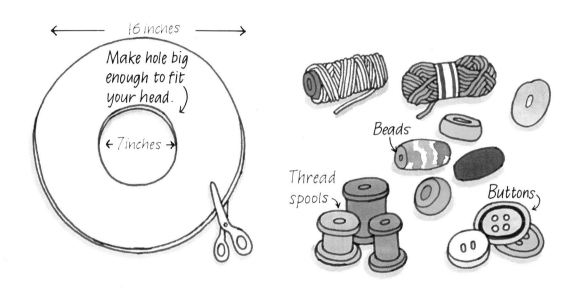

16 inches

Make hole big enough to fit your head.

7 inches

Thread spools

Beads

Buttons

1 Draw a circle on card. Then draw a smaller one in the center. Cut both out.

2 Collect lots of different things to thread onto wool or string.

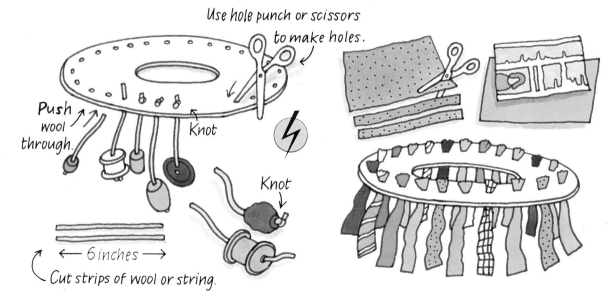

Use hole punch or scissors to make holes.

Push wool through.

Knot

Knot

6 inches

Cut strips of wool or string.

3 Make holes around the brim. Thread the objects and push the wool through the holes.

You could use strips of material or paper instead of wool or string. Don't knot, just pull the ends through.

Make a festival hat with tinsel. If you make small holes, you won't need to knot the ends – just pull a little bit through.

You can tie anything you like on to the hat. Try small plastic toys, jewelry or curtain rings.

If you like, use some short strings and some long.

Edge of hat

Pirate

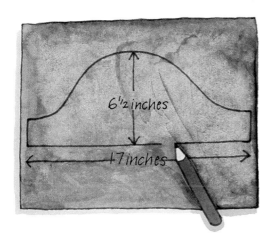

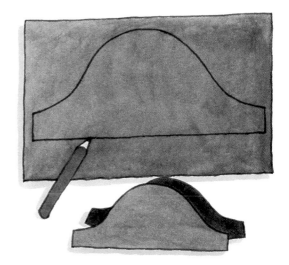

1 Draw the shape of a "Captain Hook" pirate hat onto thick, black paper.

6½ inches

17 inches

2 Cut it out, then draw around it on black paper again. Cut out the second shape.

3 Draw a skull and crossbones on white paper. Cut them out.

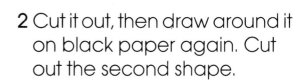

Glue

4 Stick on the skull and crossbones. Glue the two pieces together at the ends.

Here's another hat for one of Captain Hook's crew.

You need a scarf or square of material and two curtain rings.

Tie the scarf around your head. Mark it above each ear and sew rings on.

Make an eye patch out of black paper glued over thin elastic.

Fold → over

← Glue

You could safety pin a soft toy parrot to one shoulder.

Crown

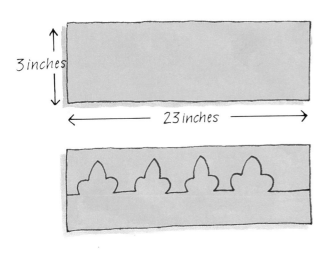

3 inches

23 inches

Cut along the pattern.

Glue

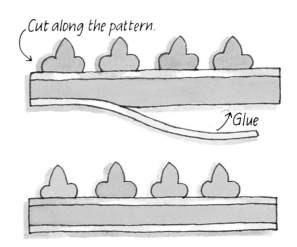

1 Cut out a strip of gold or yellow card. Draw the crown shape and cut it out.

2 Cut two thin strips out of silver paper and glue them on the crown.

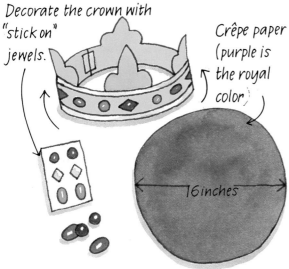

Decorate the crown with "stick on" jewels.

Crêpe paper (purple is the royal color)

16 inches

Pieces of tape

Tape

Gather the crêpe paper

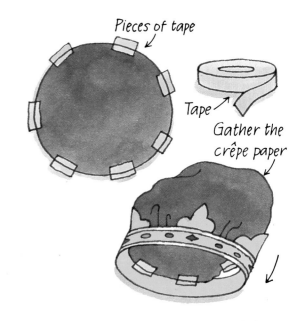

3 Bend the crown and tape the inside. Cut a circle out of crêpe or tissue paper.

4 Tape the crêpe circle inside the crown.

12

You could try lots of
different crown shapes.

"Stick on" jewels look good
on any shape of crown.

Ask if you can
borrow some
jewelry
to wear.

Headdress

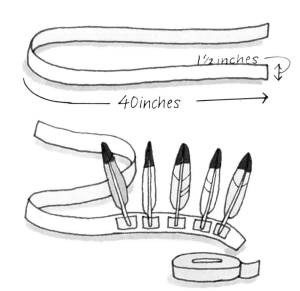

1 Collect lots of feathers and paint the tips black. Leave them to dry.

2 Cut a long strip of tape or material and glue or tape the feathers to it.

☆ Also use this instruction for the veil idea shown on page 23.

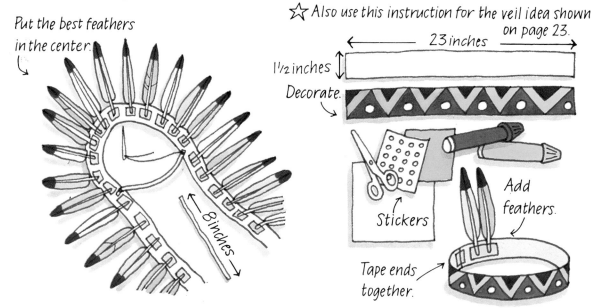

Put the best feathers in the center.

23 inches

1½ inches

Decorate.

Stickers

Add feathers.

8 inches

Tape ends together.

3 Fold the tape in two. Then sew a piece of elastic to the two sides.

You can make a simpler headdress. Use a band of thick paper or material.

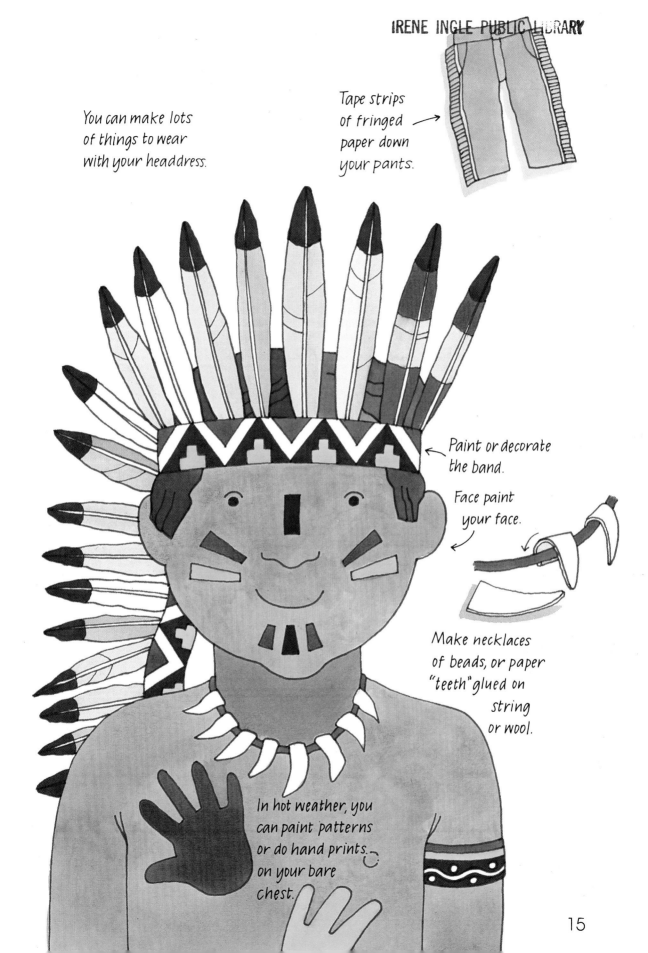

You can make lots of things to wear with your headdress.

Tape strips of fringed paper down your pants.

Paint or decorate the band.

Face paint your face.

Make necklaces of beads, or paper "teeth" glued on string or wool.

In hot weather, you can paint patterns or do hand prints on your bare chest.

15

Cap

1 Paint a bright pattern on a piece of thick paper. Let the paint dry

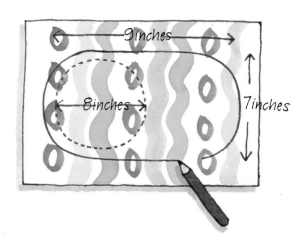

2 Draw a rectangle with rounded ends. Then draw a circle.

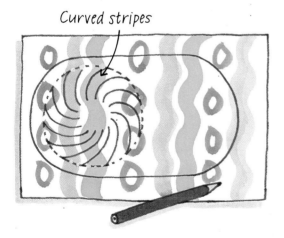

Curved stripes

3 Carefully draw the curved stripes on the circle in pencil.

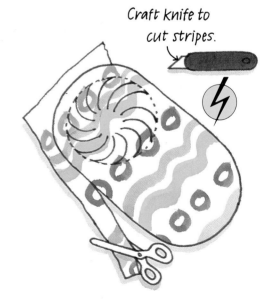

Craft knife to cut stripes.

4 Cut very carefully along the stripes. Lastly, cut out the cap shape.

Here are some ideas for decorating your cap.

Stick on some eyes to make a duck or frog.

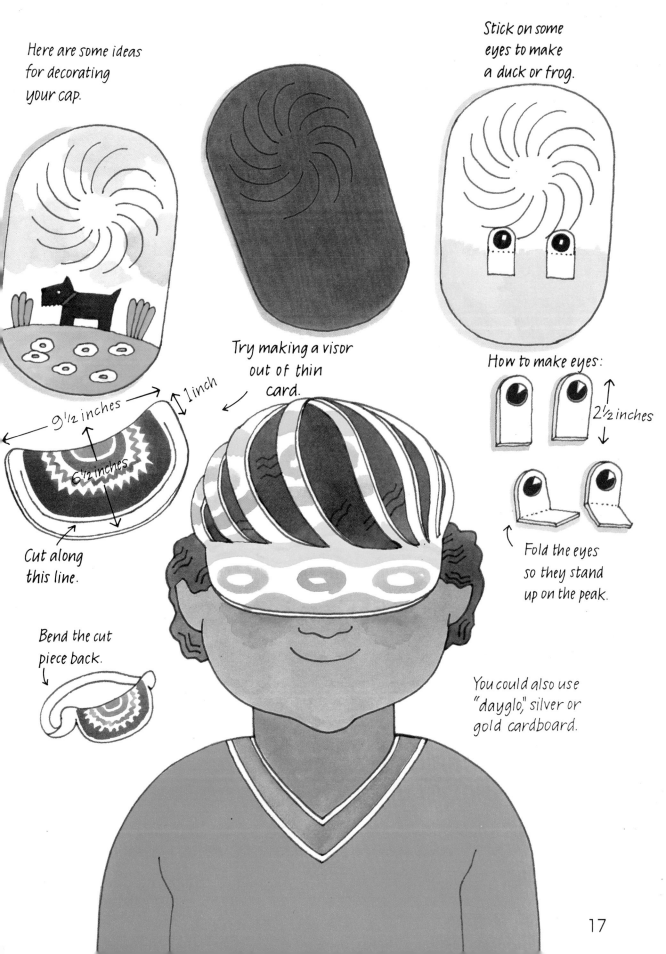

Try making a visor out of thin card.

9½ inches

1 inch

6½ inches

Cut along this line.

How to make eyes:

2½ inches

Fold the eyes so they stand up on the peak.

Bend the cut piece back.

You could also use "dayglo," silver or gold cardboard.

Flowery

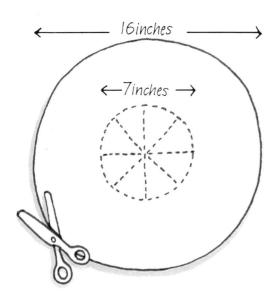

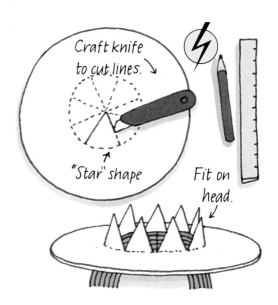

1 Draw a circle on stiff paper and cut it out. Draw a small circle in the center.

2 Draw four lines across the center of the small circle. Carefully cut along the lines.

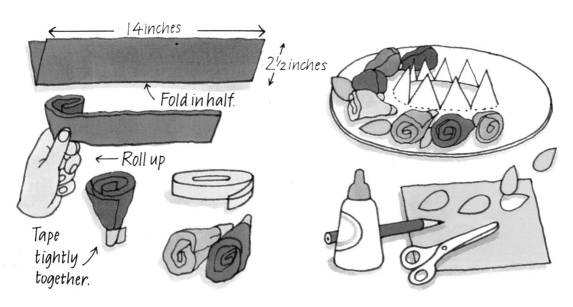

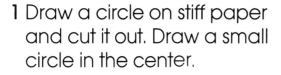

3 Use tissue paper for the flowers. Fold a long strip in half and then roll it up.

4 Make flowers in different colors. Glue them around the brim. Add some leaves.

You can make lots of different kinds of flowers. Cut the strips of tissue paper into other shapes. Roll them up as before.

Stick some paper "stamens" in the middle of the flower.

Make an extra flower and safety pin it on your chest.

Clown

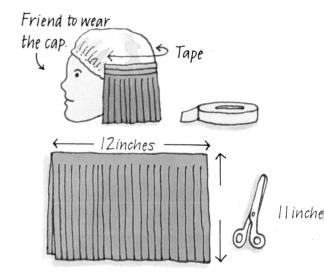

Plastic shower cap

Friend to wear the cap.

Tape

16½ inches

6½ inches

12 inches

11 inches

1 Cut out some orange crêpe paper. Fold it in half and then cut into a fringe.

2 Tape it onto the cap. Next make another longer but narrower fringe.

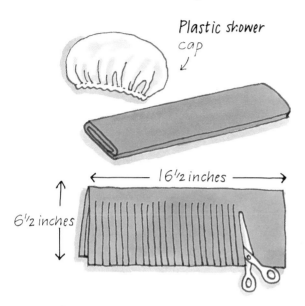

Tape

Open

3 Open the fringe and tape the middle onto the cap, like a center parting.

Card

Knot

Hole

Elastic to fit under your chin.

4 Lastly, make a tiny hat. Stick a yogurt pot onto a cardboard circle and decorate it.

You could decorate the hat with sticky shapes or cover it with colorful wrapping paper and paint the brim.

This wig looks good made out of old newspapers or magazines. If you use more paper the wig will be thicker.

Paint a clown face with face paints.

You could also make a cardboard bow on thin elastic.

More ideas

If you enjoyed making the main hats, try a few more!

There are no step-by-step instructions for these hats but you can use many of the same techniques as the main hats. Look back at the page number shown in a circle like this: ⑯

Some of the extra ideas go well with some of the main ideas if you are looking for something to wear with a friend to a party.

Painted cotton ears

Use face paints to paint a nose and whiskers.

Lion
Gather crêpe paper and fix it around a paper tie.

"Stick on" stars

Glitter

Tiara ⑫
Glue gold or silver cardboard onto a hairband. Decorate it.

Cotton→

Cut box in half and then cut the train shape.

Train
Make from a cereal packet, cut into a train shape.

Use sticks or wire for stems.

Add a top if you want.

Paint the card.

Glue paper flowers and leaves inside.

Tape or staple together.

Vase ⑱
Stick a wide band of paper together. Fill it with flowers.

Veil ⑭
Glue net around the inside of a band of cardboard.

Copy the crown hat, but use a larger circle of crêpe paper.

Chef ⑫
Glue white crêpe paper inside a band of thin cardboard.

Daisy
Sew crêpe paper petals onto a paper tie.

Tape cut out animals around hat.

Tape paper insects on to wire.

Stick straw on brim.

Easter bonnets ⑱
You can make eggs, chickens, rabbits, and flowers.

Use a straw hat as a base. Cover in paper shapes.

Streamers

Small balloons

Wrap matchboxes for presents.

Pipe cleaner fish bones

Plastic bottle

Tape paper flies onto wire.

Party time ⑱
Cover a hat shape in silver paper. Decorate for a party.

Junk
Fill a band of corrugated cardboard with newspaper.